FIRST ONE HUNDRED

Future Chron Universe

Volume 22

To The Stars Series

Book 1

D.W. PATTERSON

Eleventh Printing – May, 2023

Eleventh Printing – May, 2023

1

It was a historic undertaking. A mission to establish the first human colony on an exoplanet, a planet outside the Solar System, and Jerome was worried. He was about to undergo a test which would determine his suitability for the mission.

He would soon suit up for an extra vehicular activity (EVA), a spacewalk. But what a spacewalk. Because the crew wheel of the spaceship was located two-thirds of the way along the ship's spine from the fusion engines the "walk" to the engines would be about two thousand feet.

That's over four thousand feet, thought Jerome, *there and back.*

He wasn't actually a member of the ship's permanent crew, but a mission specialist enlisted by the ship operator just for this mission, so he didn't have a lot of EVA experience. Jerome shook his head and suited up.

The ship was the largest ever outfitted with the wormhole generator. The generator was a device that could open the near mouth of a wormhole while also "casting" or creating the far or destination mouth of the wormhole. At the same time the exotic mass, also created by the generator, would keep the wormhole stable while the ship passed through.

One could think of the generator as a way to reach into the sub-microscopic quantum topology of the universe and enlarge an existing but short-lived wormhole mouth to a useful size and duration. The generator would then cast the other mouth of the wormhole through sub-microscopic spacetime to the desired far location and enlarge it. The exotic energy-mass then lined the wormhole like the scaffolding of a bridge. Once the wormhole was established a ship, entering the near-side mouth, traveled through the wormhole dimension and out the other mouth several light years away at a speed less than the speed of light, at least in the wormhole frame of reference. None of the known laws of physics were violated by the generator, but as yet all the physics of wormholes hadn't been discovered. As with many technologies, it so often happens that humans learn to use a technology without fully understanding it.

Anyway, Jerome was a fully qualified fusion engineer and it was his job to take care of the fusion engines needed to fly the ship through normal space and that job included EVA's past the storage areas and to the distant fusion engines all the way at the back of the ship.

Okay, here goes, thought Jerome as he and Winslow accessed the airlock. Winslow, whom Jerome usually called Homer, was another rookie fusion engineer on his first interstellar mission. Though they had both served on fusion freighters in the Centauri System, neither had flown interstellar.

"You read me Homer," asked Jerome over the comm-link.

"Roger," replied Winslow, "let's get this done." The spine of the ship was made of interlinked girders of a carbon composite that was strong but flexible. The composite was wrapped in a particle shield, inside of which was an x-ray shield. This design prevented most fast-moving interstellar particles from impacting the frame and weakening it over time. Closer to the fusion engines it also prevented any radiation damage. But as Jerome and Winslow began their walk down the access bridge they knew they hadn't such good protection.

Even though the fusion engines were aneutronic they still could give off some radiation, mostly in the form of various fast-moving particles or gamma rays. These collided with the reactor shielding leaving only soft x-rays. But even at the lesser radiation a crew member would not want to remain in the vicinity too long.

Jerome hoped that they would only be there momentarily as they logged the levels of the fusion fuel supply tanks. The walk was going smoothly. Jerome was calming down and thinking to himself how easy it all was.

As they approached the storage tanks Winslow asked, "Jerome you want to take the ones on the right and I'll do the left?"

"Roger that Homer."

The *Daedalus Unbound* was a fourth-plus generation fusion ship. It's engines worked on the deuterium-helium 3 fusion reaction. The advantage of this reaction was a large amount of energy with almost an absence of neutrons. The lack of neutrons allowed a much longer engine life due to the reduction of materials damage and activation levels (radioactivity) when compared to other fusion reactions. In the fourth generation-plus engine the loss of efficiency to neutron and x-ray emissions was almost nil.

The tanks containing the deuterium oxide pellets were on the left, the tanks containing helium 3 on the right. It wasn't long until Jerome and Winslow had recorded the values from each of the tanks.

They met back at the walkway and started their return trip. Everything was going fine until Jerome looked up from the walkway to the rotating crew wheel. That's when he started getting anxious. The view was dominated by the spinning crew wheel, and just beyond it the even more magnificent but frightening spinning end cap of the huge, eight mile in diameter Logan space habitat. The habitat dominated the horizon, and the horizon was rotating!

Jerome felt a deepening sense of vertigo. He froze in his tracks and dropped to his knees as he had been trained. He activated the comm-link and called Winslow's name. Winslow had turned and was almost back to him when the fuel loading crane started to pivot silently, slow at first but gaining speed towards the two men.

Winslow keyed his mic, "Control we have a prob ..."

Those were his last words as the arm caught him and swept him from the walkway. Jerome took a glancing blow and was knocked on his back. He called after Homer and tried to rise before blacking out.

"I don't understand it," said Captain Young. "We have enough security cameras on this ship to surveil a small city and you are telling me Lieutenant that we have no vid of this incidence?"

"Unfortunately that's true ma'am," said Lt. Aaron. "Those cameras were down at the time."

"So we know nothing about what happened to engineer Winslow?"

"I'm afraid not Captain. Not until engineer Jackson wakes up and tells us what he knows."

"Very well Lieutenant, thank you for the briefing," said the Captain somewhat sarcastically.

A day later Jerome woke up.

"How's Homer?" he asked the nurse.

"Mr. Winslow's body has been recovered," she said quietly.

"Oh," said Jerome and closed his eyes again.

It was a week before Jerome felt strong enough to go before the inquiry board.

The Captain was the first to question him.

"Thank you engineer for agreeing to testify. And let me say for all here that we are sorry for the loss of your friend, engineer Winslow."

"Thank you ma'am."

"Tell us engineer what you remember about the incident."

"I remember Homer, that's what I called engineer Winslow. Homer and me had turned to walk back to the airlock.

Everything was going well until I looked up and saw the spinning crew wheel and farther on the spinning habitat. Then I felt dizzy and dropped to my knees. Next thing I know I'm knocked on my back and black out."

"So you don't remember engineer Winslow returning to your aid?"

"No ma'am I never saw him."

"And you don't remember seeing what hit you?"

"No ma'am, it happened so fast that I was still looking down at the walkway trying to recover my balance."

"Any other questions?" asked the Captain looking around the table.

Seeing that there were no more questions she thanked Jerome and dismissed him.

"Well he didn't tell us anything new," said Lieutenant Commander Rollins.

"I think he told us all he knew though," said Chief Carlos.

"I believe so too," said the Lt. Commander. "But what I don't understand is how little we know. It seems to me that all the information we should have was suppressed by someone."

"Or something," said the Captain.

The Chief and Lt. Commander stared at Captain Young.

“Anyway,” said Captain Young. “What do we do with engineer Jackson?”

“I don't think he should be allowed to continue,” said the Chief.

“I disagree,” said Lt. Commander Rollins. “A momentary dizziness which was induced by the environment and not an inherent physical problem is no reason to deny him this mission. He did what he was supposed to do. He dropped to his knees to wait for the dizziness to pass.”

“Engineer Jackson is extremely well qualified to go on this mission,” said the Captain. “I think it would be a great loss, so I agree with the Lt. Commander, sorry Chief.”

The Chief shrugged and said, “As long as we restrict his EVA opportunities.”

The other two nodded in agreement.

The *Daedalus Unbound* was held up for two weeks while the United Space Services Organization (USSO), which was a conglomeration of private companies and public offices, worked with law enforcement from the habitat to determine what had happened.

Eventually there wasn't enough evidence to rule other than accidental death and the case was closed.

2

Besides the spaceship crew whose main job was to get the *Daedalus* to its destination there was also the one-hundred settlers to be accommodated. The settlers that would go were being chosen by the Social Science Division of the USSO.

From a psychological standpoint choosing the first one hundred, the first humans ever to try to settle an exoplanet, was difficult because the mission had two conflicting goals; getting there and surviving there.

Getting there could be compared to the early treks across the frozen polar regions back on Earth where individuals were faced with a situation that precluded group activity except maybe coordination over rough terrain. Highly autonomous individuals were happy crossing the polar regions and were also happy to be alone, uninterested in accommodating others in a group.

But a group was all important once the settlement building commenced. In group dynamics extraversion, agreeableness and conscientiousness became highly prized attributes. All these attributes contributed to constructive communication and cooperation which task oriented individual's lacked.

So if the psychologists chose only one type of individual then that part of the mission would have a greater chance of success but the other part would have a greater chance of failure. Maybe a half-half choice would be best? But then there was the possibility of developing distinct subcultures which could drift apart because of different goals and values. The specter of serious conflict between the two groups became a very real concern since tensions between such groups had been noted since the dawn of space travel.

Dr. Leonard Maslen, head of the psychology department, was discussing the psychological factors that would affect the flight with his colleague Dr. Christina Maccoby who would accompany the mission. They had agreed to call the two groups trekkers and stayers.

"I agree Christina, there is definitely a spectrum of types sometimes. And it is hard to decide exactly which bin to place a settler in."

"I've been thinking Leonard that maybe that is not so bad. What do you think of a thirty-forty-thirty mix? Thirty percent trekkers, thirty percent stayers, and forty percent individuals with a mixed profile?"

"Sounds interesting and it might work. I'll run it through my model. I think it may be a good solution to a difficult sorting problem. That way we can always have approximately seventy percent well or somewhat well prepared for the segment of the mission that they are currently undertaking."

"I agree Leonard," said Dr. Maccoby smiling.

"Good then I think we've found a solution. If it holds up in simulation I'll tell corporate," said Dr. Maslen.

Later that week Glynn Kranz, Mission Director, was on his weekly walk-about visiting the different departments. He was currently visiting Dr. Maslen.

"Training," said Kranz.

"Of course, we have that already in our recommendations," said Dr. Maslen.

"Not enough," said Kranz. "You need to keep these people busy in some training scenario from the time they come on board until launch and even after."

"But Glynn, spaceship design has advanced a great deal as we've taken into account attribution error. We now design for the right 'type' of social and environmental factors and not the right 'type' of person."

"That's as may be Doctor but it doesn't hurt to reinforce their character as well."

"That's the old 'right stuff' argument Glynn. That went out with chemical rockets. There have been many fundamental studies showing that 'good' people can be manipulated into doing 'bad' things under the right situational circumstances."

"Well that 'old right stuff' as you call it got us into space, to the moon and to Mars. So I wouldn't dismiss it off hand."

Kranz had been handling space missions all his life, even before he graduated from school. Now with the USSO Kranz had overall responsibility for the settlement mission to the Trilos System.

USSO was based out of the Logan Settlement orbiting Alpha Centauri B. This mission would be the first to establish a settlememnt on a solid body. Until now all extra-solar settlements had been in the Centauri System and in cylinder shaped space habitats.

But what habitats! Logan itself was a dual cylinder habitat. Each cylinder was 8 miles in diameter and some 40 miles in length. One cylinder was residential and commercial with almost 5 million people and the other was light industrial and agricultural. Each cylinder rotated to provide eight-tenths of Earth gravity. Rigidly attached at their end-caps the oppositely rotating cylinders canceled the angular moment of the entire structure making it easier to keep it aligned with Alpha Centauri B. A fixed alignment also assisted in keeping the light reflecting mirrors illuminating the interior properly.

Other habitats also orbited Centauri B and Centauri A. Enough habitats of all sizes so that nearly three hundred million people now populated the system.

Kranz left the social sciences and was on his way to the engineering building to meet with the Head of Spacecraft Engineering.

"Hey Glynn, how are you?"

"Fine Sergei, how about you?"

"Same Glynn."

"Sergei I came to discuss the *Daedalus*. Can you give me an update?"

"Well at this time the spacecraft is set to undergo its first test flight next month. The wheel section is already rotating."

"I know, at a thousand feet in diameter it's quite a sight to see," said Kranz. "And you integrated the layers of the wormhole generator well."

"Yeah the inner layer where the large mass is exposed when the outer layer creates the Mach effect was the key. Once we had it attached securely it was easy to add the other two layers. Still the next layer, the actuator layer, the layer that drives the outer layer and the Mach effect, that was a bit tricky at this scale. It's still a piezoelectric but we had to figure out how to stiffen it without compromising its performance."

"I've always been surprised at how relatively simple is the structure of the generator," said Kranz. "I mean the material science and the power engineering are impressive but three layers of material slowly spinning," he shook his head. "I would never have expected such an arrangement would make a wormhole."

"Yeah Elias Mach was a pretty smart kid when he developed the generator. Who would have thought that you could shield a local mass from the universal mass and thereby unlock the intrinsic mass of the electron? And that the intrinsic electron mass would be huge and negative which is exactly what is needed to create and maintain a wormhole. I mean the theories were there but it was genius to pull them all together and build something practical."

"Still it has to be spinning to work. And that's a big wheel to spin," said Kranz.

"Yeah we've never spun anything that big at one point-seven revolutions a minute to get the four-tenths gravity we want. The outer surface of that big wheel will be moving at almost one-hundred kilometers per hour."

"You think it will hold together?"

"It should, it's designed to spin as fast as two and a half revolutions per minute. So I don't expect any structural problems. We'll be looking at the bearing loads though, where it attaches to the fuselage of the ship."

"It's magnificent Sergei."

Kranz paused a moment. "I suppose you've been in contact with the psychologists?"

"Yes I have," said Sergei Prokiev.

"They've presented you with the environmental requirements?"

"Yes we will accommodate them."

"How about project delays as a result?"

"They shouldn't be severe. We will simply move some walls around so that every one of the crewmen will have a windowed view in their quarters."

"Apartment Sergei, don't forget."

"Yes their terminology is unusual for our industry. But if it gives the mission a better chance at success, then I'm willing to conform my spacecraft. And myself for that matter," he said with a smile.

"You've always been a team player Sergei. That's why you are the best."

3

Six weeks later the *Daedalus Unbound* was preparing for departure and the settlers were boarding to occupy their assigned quarters or apartments. The apartments were spacious compared to previous fusion spaceships. The recommendations of the environmental psychologists had been taken seriously. Four hundred square feet apartments, each with a small porthole window, seemed even roomier than their square footage would suggest. The three rooms included a ten by twenty living room-kitchen, a ten by twelve bedroom and an eight by ten bathroom. The kitchen included a small fridge and food processing center. Except for the reduced gravity it might have been any hotel room back in the habitat.

"This is nice, much nicer than the simulations we've been through," said Lauren.

"Yeah, if it was just a bit larger it would be like back home," said Grace.

Lauren Bremen and Grace Patrick had come aboard the *Daedalus* to stow their personal belongings and prepare for the launch. Lauren was an astronomer and Grace an operating room nurse.

"Oh look, a window," said Lauren.

"I don't know why," said Grace. "With the wallscreen you can pretty much see anything you want."

"Yeah but it's nicer sometimes to see the 'real world' you know?"

“I guess so,” said Grace as she turned on the wallscreen and said, “Logan Habitat, inside axis view.”

The entire wall filled with a real-time image of the inside of the habitat. The shot was from a camera along the axis. The image was spinning.

“Stop spin,” said Grace.

The video stopped spinning, or rather the software compensated for the spin so as to show a stationary image. A vista of the cylindrical colony almost to the far end was shown by a camera several hundred feet above “ground” level. The curvature of the long cylinder was clearly seen as the sides rose up and out of the picture. There was a noticeable tilt to the taller buildings as the camera pivoted from one side to the other.

“That's nice Grace but I still like having a window, however small, to look out of.”

Grace turned back to the wallscreen and said, “Off.” The screen became a wall again. “Oh look,” she said, “a small fridge and a food processing center. That will be great for those long days when I'm too tired from work to go out to a restaurant.”

“I agree,” said Lauren. “Sometimes just a quick snack and curl up on the couch in front of the wallscreen is what I really need. Did you give them your list of VR vids you wanted?”

“Yeah,” said Grace, “but I'm also bringing a few on my Emmie which are just for me, if you know what I mean.”

“Oh sure,” said Lauren with a grin.

An Emmie was a personal assistant device that most people carried. It contained a form of artificial intelligence derived from a human brain scan. (Em, from the word emulation, was the brain scan running in a computer. Ems provided much of the processing power in the settlements for monitoring, running machinery, robots and many other devices. Ems were organized into "families." A scan could be copied or "budded," as the Ems called it, as many times as necessary for an Em family to fulfill its employment contract. These buds could be continued or retired after the job was finished, depending on the Em family's finances. Ems were ubiquitous in society and had been so for several centuries).

Grace and Lauren continued their tour of the *Daedalus* by viewing the restaurants, the gym, the theater, the different stores and finally the medical facilities where Grace would be working.

"Well," said Lauren, "I for one am impressed. I don't think I will have any problem fitting in."

"Yes," said Grace, "it is impressive. I suppose if one is going to settle a new planet this isn't a bad way to go."

They continued their stroll along the corridors of the *Daedalus* with many bots rushing by but few people.

A man was just exiting from his quarters as Lauren and Grace passed by.

"Good day ladies," he said. "I'm Jerome Jackson one of the fusion engineers."

“Oh hi,” said Lauren, “I'm Lauren Bremen, astronomer, and this is my friend Grace Patrick, she's an operating room nurse. I've seen you in the training sessions I think.”

“No doubt,” said Jerome, “those were required. Will you ladies be at the pre-launch party tonight?”

“That's our plans,” said Grace.

“Excellent,” said Jerome with a smile. “I'll be asking each of you for a dance. See you there, bye.”

“Bye,” said Grace and Lauren almost at the same time.

When Jerome was out of hearing range Grace said, “Cute but flirty.”

“Flirty is okay as long as he knows the limits,” said Lauren.

Grace nodded.

The pre-launch party was in full swing. Lauren and Grace had danced with Jerome and many others. The settlers on the *Daedalus* were almost equally male and female. There were fifteen couples, the rest were single. The sexual preferences of all were known by the psychologists and taken into account in the crew make-up. All were under sixty in a society where life expectancy was more than two times that. Pregnancies were strictly prohibited until landfall.

It was approaching midnight when the Captain of the *Daedalus*, Wilma Young, called for attention.

“Please, please ladies and gentlemen may I have your attention.”

The crowd quieted.

"Thank you. As you know this is our last night docked to the habitat. Tomorrow evening we will be departing, so you have less than eighteen hours to make your final preparations. But before I dismiss the party let me just say this. We have probably the finest spaceship ever built and I believe the best crew. We have the wormhole drive which will make our voyage relatively quick considering the forty light-years we have to go. We have everything we need to make this mission a success.

"But we have no guarantee. Even though things may seem to be going smoothly we are going into the unknown. And because it is unknown it could offer a challenge we are not trained for. Training only goes so far. I am depending on all of you to not only do your jobs but to be creative and inventive and to not be afraid to tackle the challenges we will face head-on. That is why the USSO is sending humans and not just robots. Let us show them, the Centauri System, and even those back in the old Solar System, that men and women can still be the key to a successful mission.

"Thank-you."

After a long round of applause the party goers eventually drifted away to their rooms to sleep.

4

The *Daedalus Unbound* was on its way. The ship had launched late the day after the party. Mostly automated, it hadn't required many crew to be present. Accelerating and then decelerating at point-four Earth gravity it would take the ship a couple of weeks to put enough distance between it and the Centauri System before it could use its wormhole drive safely.

The concentration of energy required to open a wormhole was so great that to chance its use closer than ten AU (about the distance from the Sun to Saturn) from any human habitat was unwise. As had been discovered by accident two decades earlier, if enough energy was concentrated at a point in space a dangerous disruption of spacetime would occur, and that disruption would propagate at the speed of light destroying any mass in its way. Fortunately the effect dissipated over distance and ten AU was thought to be an adequate safety quarantine for a normal "jump".

During acceleration and deceleration the wheel section would not be spinning and the living quarters would be turned, like beads on a string, so that the applied force, the acceleration, was in the proper direction. The resulting artificial gravity allowed the crew and the settlers to eat, sleep and do other mundane chores necessary in a normal manner on the spaceship.

Settlers were also encouraged during this phase of the voyage to become acquainted and seek out fellow settlers or crew members with similar interests in hobbies, games and other diverse social activities.

Some, such as Grace, were convinced by their co-workers, in this case one of the two doctors in the medical group, to join a band he was putting together with the mission's psychologist, Dr. Maccoby. Grace would play the piano.

Others such as Lauren had joined a writer's group with five others. She was also spending her time testing the telescopes and computer systems for the observations she would be making around the stars the *Daedalus* would be visiting in its hop-scotch mission plan. Because of the distance limitations of the wormhole drive and the safety concerns over energy concentration, seven light years for a single jump was the permitted limit. So to get to its destination, the star system previously known as WISE 0735 and now known as Trilos, the ship would need to make several jumps.

Once it arrived in the vicinity of a star, the isotopic energy reservoir banks, which provided the huge amount of energy the wormhole drive demanded, would be renewed by orbiting the star for a number of days and recharging on its radiation. Isotopic energy storage used the atomic nucleus rather than chemical means. The resulting energy concentration was magnitudes greater than any previous system. An assist from the fusion engines would help to shorten the charging time.

Jerome hadn't joined any social group. He still hadn't completely gotten over the loss of Homer and anyway he was too busy doing shift work in the engineering department. The fusion engine was in the midst of its first long run.

Four years of college two years of graduate work, four years of a doctorate and here I am standing an eight hour shift that any bright technician could manage. Somethings wrong somewhere.

"Hey Jerome," said Freddie Reynolds. "You got that data yet?"

Freddie Reynolds was younger than Jerome but was already a shift supervisor.

"Yeah, here it is," said Jerome handing Freddie his Emmie. "I've already looked it over. I don't like the numbers."

"What do you mean?"

"They're different than simulation."

"Is that really a surprise?" asked Freddie. "I mean we expected some difference."

"I know Freddie but these numbers are much different."

"What do the fusion Emmies say?"

"They say that the engine is working within parameters. But why wouldn't they say that? They're responsible for its operation."

"Jerome, we've been flying with these fusion Emmies for what? Hundreds of years? At least since the second generation fusion ships. They should know how to manage a fusion rocket by now. Don't you think?"

"I know," said Jerome with exasperation. "But do me a favor?"

"What?"

"Ask the Chief to look it over."

"I'll express your concerns to the Chief," said Freddie as he turned to walk away.

Jerome hadn't heard anything from the Chief of Engineering so he kept quiet about the anomaly until one day in the deli where he was eating a late lunch. He had made his soup and salad, or rather the food processing center had made them from his input, then turned to find a seat and saw Lauren eating by herself.

"Hi Lauren," said Jerome walking up to her table. "You're eating late aren't you?"

"Oh hi Jerome please join me. Yeah, I decided to finish my scope calibrations rather than break off for lunch. Once I start them it's easier to keep going than restarting. How about you?"

Jerome sat down and said, "Supervisor's changing my shift again. I don't know if I'm eating a late lunch, early dinner or something else. I just know I'm hungry."

"Rotating shift work, that's tough. So that's why I haven't seen you around the past week."

"Yeah, while the engines are running we are hard pressed to oversee operations."

"I thought the Emmies would have made that easy?"

"Well," said Jerome looking around the empty room. "You see Lauren I don't know if I should tell you this but I feel someone should know."

He paused.

"Understand I've told my superiors and they've said nothing about keeping it quiet but ..."

"Jerome you have to tell me now, you've got me worried."

"Oh I'm sorry Lauren, it's nothing to be worried about I assure you. It's just ..."

"Jerome!"

"Okay, quiet, not so loud. You see I was running engine performance data through my personal Emmie and the results I got disagree with what the fusion Emmies are telling me."

Lauren looked shocked, "I don't see how that is possible Jerome."

Jerome sank back in his chair, "That's the way my supervisor, Freddie Reynolds felt also. He refused to believe me."

"Oh I believe you're getting different results Jerome. But are you sure you are using the same analysis program as the fusion Emmies?"

"That's where I got the program."

"Could something be wrong with your Emmie?"

"I doubt it but let's try an experiment. Let me send the program and data to yours and let's see if we get the same results."

"Okay," said Lauren.

Within a couple of minutes the program and data were exchanged and the results were displayed on both Emmies.

"See," said Jerome imploringly.

"I see. I don't understand what they mean but the numbers are the same."

"Good," said Jerome smiling, "I'm not crazy then. As far as what they mean. They mean that we are burning a lot more helium 3 than the fusion Emmies say we are. The efficiency of the engines is off and the fusion Emmies haven't been able to correct the problem."

"So they are lying to us to cover up their failure? I thought that was impossible for an Emmie?"

"Not impossible but extremely rare. I know of only a couple of cases in the past where Emmies were found to have lied, or at least withheld the whole truth, but neither one of those involved fusion Emmies."

"So what will happen Jerome if you're right and they are wrong?

"We'll run out of fusion fuel long before we reach Trilos."

"What will happen then?" said Lauren worriedly.

"Don't worry. We should be able to still use the wormhole drive to call for help. Then we just wait to be rescued," said Jerome with a forced smile.

5

Regardless of Jerome's worries the mission seemed to be going off without a hitch. The *Daedalus* had already put two star systems behind it with five more to go before it arrived at Trilos. The ship had come out of its wormhole and entered an orbit around the star LHS 828, a red dwarf, nearly six days before.

Lauren was finishing up her observations of the star and its associated planetary system. Besides the Jupiter sized planet that astronomers had long suspected she had also found a sub-Jupiter sized planet orbiting a little further out and a rocky planet orbiting closer in. A tenuous asteroid belt was also discovered beyond the farthest gas giant. Lauren would soon be making a report and sending it back to Centauri through a wormhole enabled communication link.

The recharging of the isotopics was almost complete and everyone was preparing for the next jump which would take them to their halfway point the brown dwarf star labeled DENIS J081740 on the star maps. It was a small star only fifteen times the mass of Jupiter with a surface temperature of only one-thousand kelvins. Because of its low surface temperature and the need to recharge the isotopics after the jump, the stay around DENIS J081740 would be the longest of the mission.

The announcement of impending wormhole generator engagement came over Lauren's Emmie. She and Grace were in her quarters with the wallscreen on and a view of the space directly in front of the ship. There they saw the small point of light resembling a distance star begin to form. But this star grew in size becoming brighter and brighter.

The ship's frame groaned as the Mach effect was established and shielded the inner layer from the universal mass.

The physics of the effect was simple arithmetic. What was known as the measured mass of the electron was actually a combination of its intrinsic mass and the mass of the large cloud of virtual particles surrounding it. Since the measured value was small and negative, and it was known that the mass of the virtual particles was large and positive then the intrinsic mass of the electron had to be large and negative to balance out.

The Mach effect simply screened the inner layer's electrons from the mass of the rest of the universe. Thereby exposing not only a huge mass but also a negative mass (because of the arithmetic) sometimes called exotic because it exerted a repulsive gravitational force on ordinary mass. This energy or mass density was enough to open the mouth of a microscopic wormhole and the repulsive gravitational force could keep it open.

The spot of light continued to grow until it was a sphere larger than the *Daedalus* and its crew wheel. Around the sphere the stars elongated more and more until they became a halo around the wormhole's mouth. This was the effect known to astronomers as gravitational lensing, where the light behind a large mass such as the wormhole mouth was deflected around the mass.

When the mouth seemed to be a stable and fully formed sphere the ship slowly started to move toward it. The effect was as if one were immersed in a brilliant light and then almost instantly there was space and the stars again. Only if observed closely the stars were displaced somewhat from before entering the wormhole.

No one had a description of the traversal. It seemed that it only took a split second but there was no conclusive evidence of the experience because human and machine seemed to enter a kind of suspension which precluded recollection or record.

Lauren and Grace were still staring at the wallscreen.

"Well I guess its over," said Grace.

"Yeah, but something's not right," said Lauren.

"What do you mean?"

"Where's the brown dwarf? I don't see it on any of the views."

Lauren switched between the different views.

"We've never come out of a wormhole this far away from the target star."

"I see what you mean," said Grace.

The Captain had called a meeting of her officers and engineers.

"What happened Chief?"

"Ma'am as far as I can tell we came out of wormhole traverse earlier than expected."

"That's apparent Chief."

The Chief fidgeted.

"Yes ma'am. We estimate we are only two AU away. That's less than one-tenth of one percent and we can be there in a little over six days ma'am."

"As small as that may be Chief it still doesn't explain why I can't look out my wallscreen at the star we should be orbiting."

Jerome was in the meeting wondering if he should speak up. It didn't seem that anyone else even had a theory.

"Well," said Captain Young. "Does anyone have anything to say?"

Jerome squirmed in his seat. The Captain turned to look at him. He could see that while still commanding, she was also imploring anyone for help. Even a lowly engineer.

"Ma'am," said Jerome his voice almost cracking. "I have a theory that may have some bearing on this incident."

"You seem to be the only one engineer, proceed."

Jerome could see the Chief rolling his eyes, this was going to cost him.

"You see ma'am I have found a discrepancy between reported helium 3 usage and my calculations."

"Really, and you reported this?"

7

"I don't know Lauren, I just don't know," said Jerome. "Andy helped take the body into the infirmary. I thought Dr. Misner was going to start right away but I haven't heard anything."

"It's pretty hard to accept Jerome," said Lauren. She had sought Jerome out after dinner the following day. They were having coffee in the cafe.

"Jerome I have a bad feeling about what happened to Grace."

"What do you mean?"

"I mean that Grace, me, you, all of us had probably the most thorough physical in the world before being chosen for this mission. There couldn't have been anything wrong with Grace, the pre-flight physical would have caught it."

"You may be right Lauren, I know my physical was too thorough for comfort."

"So how does a young woman such as Grace who just had the most thorough physical known to mankind end up dead? Especially since so far it seems there was no foul play."

Jerome leaned in and whispered a bit too loud.

"Foul play! You don't mean what I think you mean do you?"

"Jerome," said Lauren shaking her head, "you of all people should be suspicious. You were the target of two attempts on your life."

"Yes ma'am," said Jerome not stopping for a response. "I believe that the fusion Emmies are in error and that we will run out of helium 3 before Trilos if we don't begin to conserve it."

The room exploded with shouts and accusations. The Chief was yelling straight at Jerome and pointing his finger. Freddie was protesting. Most were protesting that it was impossible.

"Quiet, quiet!" said the Captain. "You gentlemen will maintain protocol!"

The room quieted although the Chief was still pointing at Jerome.

"Chief, did the engineer report his findings to you?"

The Chief put down his arm but hesitated to respond.

"I'm asking you a direct question Mr. Carlos and I am ordering you to answer now!"

"Yes ma'am," said the Chief quietly. "But ma'am we ran a full diagnostics and found nothing wrong."

The Captain interrupted him and turned to Jerome.

"Dr. Jackson how did you come up with this, ah, theory?"

Jerome was more confident now having weathered the assault he knew would come when he reported his findings.

"Captain, I downloaded the fuel calculation program from the fusion Emmies and ran it on my Emmie and one other. Both independent Emmies came up with the same numbers and the numbers say that we are using fuel at a much higher rate than expected. There is something wrong with the efficiency of the engines and the fusion Emmies have not been able to correct it."

"Chief did you verify Dr. Jackson's procedures for yourself?"

"Well no ma'am. Like I said the diagnostics showed no problems and the readings from the fuel tanks show no unusual fuel usage."

"Ma'am," said Jerome. "The fusion Emmies could be intercepting those readings and changing them before they arrive in command."

"Hog wash!" said Chief Carlos.

The Captain held up her hand for quiet.

"Okay, I think I see what we should do. Dr. Jackson you are to choose someone to accompany you to the fuel tanks and get us a manual reading. Not a reading through your Emmie but a manual reading. Understood?"

Jerome felt his stomach turn, "Yes ma'am," he said weakly.

"Meeting dismissed," said the Captain who then stormed from the room.

Jerome was almost the last one up. *Not again*, he thought.

Jerome chose Homer's replacement, Alvin "Andy" Andrews, to go on the EVA with him. Jerome made sure Andy knew what had happened on the last space walk.

“So you really don't know what happened?” asked engineer Andrews.

“No, I was knocked on my back or shoved I don't know which and then I blacked out. When I came to I was inside the ship. Turned out my air supply had been compromised.”

“And this happened just as you were beginning to head back?”

“Yeah.”

“Well we should definitely watch ourselves at that point.”

Jerome nodded in agreement.

6

The space walk was going well. Andy had chosen to check the deuterium oxide tanks while Jerome checked the helium 3.

Just like before, thought Jerome as he opened up the access port to the manual readout.

Tapping the numbers into his Emmie.

Just as I suspected.

He called to Andy when he was finished.

"Andy you ready to head back."

"Roger."

"Okay, meet you at the walkway."

Jerome was there first with Andy not far behind. This time Jerome took the lead heading back. Even though he had promised himself he would keep his eyes on the walkway he couldn't help but look up at the spinning crew wheel, spinning as the ship had ceased motion until the readings were taken. This time it wasn't as overwhelming without the habitat in the background.

He continued walking but before he had taken a couple of steps he felt a shove from behind that sent him sprawling. When he rolled over he saw Andy standing back and the robotic fuel service arm returning to its neutral position.

"What happened Andy? Did you push me?"

"Yeah I saw the arm there swinging towards us and pushed you to keep it from hitting you."

"Okay Andy, I think you just found out what killed Homer. Let's get back and report."

The Captain had called another meeting of her crew and the engineers.

"First I'd like to thank our ship's psychologist Dr. Maccoby for sitting in. As you will see we will need her expertise."

Dr. Maccoby nodded her head in response.

"Okay we've got a couple of things we have to cover people. First, we have to establish what we should do about these fuel readings. We can't proceed with business as usual. We are going to have to make some changes in our mission plan. We may even decide we will have to scrub the mission."

A look went around the room.

"Next we have to find out how this fuel discrepancy arose and how that robotic arm decided to move just when engineers Andrews and Jackson were passing. And why we can't get any vid of this latest incidence either. There is just too much coincidence involved.

"Okay what do we do about the fuel situation?"

Seeing no immediate response was forthcoming the Captain turned to the Chief.

“Chief you want to tell us about your idea?”

“Of course Captain,” said Chief Carlos. “I've run the numbers using the readings that engineers Jackson and Andrews returned. We have enough fuel to continue the mission if we cease to use the fusion engines in the recharging operation.”

“But what does that do to the schedule?”

“It adds about one hundred thirty-five days to our schedule.”

“That means two hundred and five days rather than the seventy days of the original mission.”

“That's true ma'am but we do have the ability to generate enough food supply for an extended mission and we have all the other stores necessary.”

“Thank you Chief but I am more concerned with the impact on the crew and settlers than the ship's supplies. They, especially the settlers, didn't sign up for seven months aboard this ship. And I have to worry about keeping up their morale. Dr. Maccoby would you care to comment.”

“Thank you Captain. I would say that you should consider getting the crew and settlers to buy in to whatever decision is made.”

“Okay Doctor how would I go about doing that?”

“Well off the top of my head I would suggest that after you explain the situation to them you allow them to vote on the alternatives.”

“And if they vote to return?”

“Then Captain I would think you would want to take them back. After all you don't want to continue on such a historic mission with people that are not committed to its success. But I think I can assure you that you will get a majority voting to continue. They have been chosen for their enthusiasm and dedication.”

“Very well Doctor I will consider your advice and thank you for coming.”

Dr. Maccoby nodded and left the room.

“Okay that's handled. Now for the second problem. How did we get in this mess in the first place? Does anyone have any idea about what has happened to the fusion Emmies, the apparently homicidal robotic arm, the surveillance cams at the far end of the walkway?”

There was silence.

“Anyone?” said the Captain looking disappointedly around the room.

Jerome didn't want to do it but he raised his hand.

“Don't just raise your hand engineer speak up,” said the Captain.

“I believe Captain the same agency that miscalculated the fuel status is at work here.”

“You mean the fusion Emmies?”

"Yes ma'am."

Jerome could feel the Chief's stare.

"The fuel Emmies have priority over that section of the ship. They control the refueling arm and if needed could get control of the surveillance cam, I checked into it."

"Is this true Chief?"

"Captain it's possible but highly unlikely. There are no known incidences such as we have witnessed involving the fuel Emmies and a fusion ship. Similar incidences were always traced to human agency or error."

"The Chief is right about such incidences aboard a fusion ship," said Jerome. "But such incidences have occurred in the past involving Emmies. Shortly after the first Emmies were introduced into human society one of them was compromised to such an extent by a ruthless psychotic that the Emmie became involved in a plot to hurt and possibly kill people."

"Why haven't I ever heard of such a thing?" asked the Chief skeptically.

"It's not common knowledge in the literature Chief and safeguards were imposed after the incident to prevent it from happening again."

"This is absurd Captain," said the Chief. "I have years more training and years more experience with fusion Emmies than the engineer here and I've never heard of such a thing."

"That may be so Chief but I have experience that you don't. You see, I know about it because the targets were ancestors of mine."

"Engineer if what you say is true then we are all in imminent danger. The fusion Emmies could terminate this mission anytime with whatever loss of equipment and lives they believe is necessary," said the Captain.

There was quiet, then the Captain's Emmie alarmed.

"Yes," said the Captain.

"Captain we have a problem."

"Go ahead Lieutenant Aaron."

"Captain, Grace Patrick has been found dead."

"Where?"

"Her apartment."

"On my way," said Captain Young.

"Lt. Commander if you will follow me."

"Dismissed," she barked as she left the room.

The "crime scene" was roped off, at least the door had a warning not to enter.

Captain Young found her Security Chief and a couple of his temporary deputies inside.

"What have you found Lieutenant Aaron?" she asked as she entered.

"Just Ms. Patrick in her bed. She appears to have been dead for a few hours. Lauren Bremen called me when Grace failed to show up for lunch with Lauren and did not answer the door. As far as I can tell there's been no struggle, nothing indicates any kind of altercation in the apartment. Dr. Misner is in there now examining the body."

"Very well Lieutenant Aaron I'll just see if Dr. Misner has found anything."

Captain Young stopped at the door to the bedroom and asked, "Dr. Misner have you found anything unusual?"

"Only that there doesn't seem to be anything visibly wrong Captain."

"So the next step?" asked the Captain.

"The next step is to get the body to the infirmary and perform an autopsy. Perhaps that will tell us something."

"Very well Doctor but do one thing for me please?"

"Yes Captain?"

"Be as discreet as possible, we don't want a lot of wild stories going around."

The Doctor nodded his head.

"You mean the robotic arm incidents?"

"What did you think?" said Lauren somewhat at a loss.

"I hadn't thought much about it Lauren, I just thought they were accidents you know."

Lauren just stared.

Eventually it registered with Jerome, he opened his mouth but closed it.

"You get it now?"

"You might be right Lauren, but if all these incidents are related then someone is trying to deliberately compromise the mission."

"Deliberately compromise the mission," said Lauren averting her eyes, "that's a polite way to put it. How about killing people?"

Jerome looked distressed.

"I'm sorry Lauren I didn't mean to be so flippant. I know that Grace was your friend."

Dr. Misner downloaded the pre-programmed routines into the nanobots he would be using in the autopsy. Once injected into the body of the deceased the bots would return a plethora of information. It was unusual if they did not pinpoint the cause or causes of death.

The robotic arm injected the bots into Grace's body. A blood volume expander rich in energy for the bots had already been introduced into the body's circulatory system. The heart was caused to beat and distributed this expander throughout, allowing the nanobots to go almost anywhere searching for the cause or causes of death.

From the beating of the heart and the waste energy of the nanobots the temperature of the body started to rise. After ten minutes the bots were pooling in the temple lobes. There they were forming an antenna lattice which would be used in conjunction with the externally applied radio field to transmit the results of the autopsy to the doctor's Emmie.

Dr. Misner began to review the results, kidney failure, liver failure, heart failure, the list went on. Nearly every organ in the body had failed or been compromised as if the body had attacked itself.

Autoimmune. But there's no indication of unusual antibodies.

He sat back a minute, then he queried the Emmie. Then it dawned on him.

An aerosol.

"So if I follow what you are saying Doctor, you think someone used this same nano-technology that you used to do the autopsy?"

"That's right Captain," said Dr. Misner. "The same nanotech I used to perform the autopsy on Ms. Patrick could have been used to cause her death."

"You said could, are you not sure?"

"The autopsy nanobots found no signs of nano-technology in the body. Which is unusual nowadays. So no I can't be one hundred percent sure but I can't think of any other way to explain the autopsy results."

"Dr. Misner, could you speculate on who aboard this vessel would have the skills to manipulate such nano-technology?"

"Well, of course myself, Dr. Wilson, Dr. Maccoby probably, and maybe the engineers. That's all I can think of."

"Thank you Doctor, that's enough for now."

The Captain had called an all hands meeting in the assembly hall. The crew was sitting upfront, Jerome was with Lauren and the other settlers in the back. The Captain called the meeting to order.

"As you know we have had an unfortunate loss of life. Nurse Grace Patrick has died. As of now we are ruling it a natural death caused by an autoimmune response. But our medical team is still investigating. Let me just say that although I did not know Grace well those that did have only the highest opinion of her character and professional demeanor. The mission has lost a very important person. I understand that there will be a memorial for her at sixteen hundred hours tomorrow.

"Now to other business, some of you may already know what I have to say next but I suspect this is news to most of you. We have become aware of a problem with our fusion engines. It seems they have not been as efficient as expected. The result is that we will have to conserve our fusion fuel. This means precisely that we will no longer be able to use our engines to shorten our stay around a star. We will have to rely solely on the star's energy for charging the isotopic reservoirs.

"The result is that the mission to get to the Trilos system will take two-hundred and five days instead of the original seventy. That is if we choose to continue the mission. Since there has been such a huge change in mission duration I've decided to let you, the settlers and contractors, decide as to whether we continue the mission as planned or turn back now. The ship's permanent crew will follow my orders.

"You each will vote using your Emmie devices. Yes, we continue or no, we turn back. I give you twenty four hours from now to decide. At that time the isotopics will be recharged sufficiently to make a jump, whether that jump is towards Trilos or back towards Earth is up to you.

"Thank you, dismissed."

Jerome and Lauren had just come from Grace's memorial. They were in the coffee shop talking.

"I still don't believe it was natural causes Jerome."

"I don't know what to think Lauren. But I suspect you will be proven right in the long run. Poor Grace, how terrible."

They both sat quietly drinking their coffee.

"Have you voted yet?" asked Lauren.

"Yeah, I voted to go on. How about you?"

“Haven't voted.”

“You want to got back?”

“No, not exactly. But I would like to see that we are taking the death of Grace seriously. What happened to her could happen to any one of us if we continue. It's obvious to me anyway that someone doesn't want us to finish this mission. Who is investigating? Who are the suspects? What is being done?”

“I understand your worries Lauren but I can tell you that I've been in meetings with the Captain and from what I've seen close up I think I can state without a doubt that she is taking what happened to Grace very seriously. If there is an investigation on going, and I would be willing to bet there is, she is not going to leak the details for the obvious reason it would tip off the perpetrator.”

“You sound like a detective Jerome,” said Lauren smiling at him. “But my gut feeling tells me you are probably right about the Captain. She's not one to let loose ends go.”

Lauren was silent for a time. She unfolded her Emmie and voted.

Looking at Jerome she said, “I'm for going to Trilos.”

8

"**H**ow long did you say Chief?" asked the Captain.

"A little less than ninety days ma'am. This will be the longest stop of the mission because of the relatively weak output of the star."

"But ninety days, I wonder how the crew and settlers will pull through? I'm almost tempted to use the fusion engines to shorten the stay."

"Even if we shortened it a few days," said the Chief, "we would be endangering our rendezvous at Trilos."

"I know, I know Chief, I'm not going to do such a thing. I'm just worried about the people."

"Yes ma'am."

After the extended stay at DENIS J081740 the *Daedalus Unbound* had made the wormhole jump to the even smaller sub-brown dwarf star WISE 0536. Not much was known about WISE 0536 except that it was just barely larger than Jupiter and as a result derived most of its energy output from gravitational contraction. Being a very weak emitter of light and infrared energy the ship would have to orbit close to recharge the isotopic's for the next jump.

Lauren had been studying the "failed" star for over two weeks now. She had found something unusual. The magnetometer, used to measure the magnetic field of the star, was unusually active, an unexpected result for such an object. She was discussing her results with Jerome.

"That's right Jerome it is unusual. You usually don't see this level of activity in such an object."

"That's great," said Jerome, "you're discovery will be a real contribution to the science of brown dwarfs Lauren."

"That's all true Jerome but that's not what concerns me at the moment."

"Then what is it Lauren?"

"We are very close to this star Jerome. These strong magnetic fields could cause it to flare in the x-ray. Do you know what that means this close up?"

"It means trouble," said Jerome.

The *Dadaelus Unbound*, after almost three months of endless orbiting, was only a week away from a complete charge of the isotopics when Captain Young went missing.

Lt. Commander Rollins had to take command. He had immediately organized a search party which involved most of those onboard who weren't serving a watch or otherwise occupied.

"It shouldn't be long," said the Lt. Commander. "The ship is not that big. I've got at least thirty people searching."

"Yes sir," said the Chief. "But it is unbelievable to me that she could just disappear without a trace. I mean, the Captain?"

"We've been lax Chief. Orbiting this miserable dwarf star for almost three months has almost driven everyone crazy. It's really impacted our efficiency, I can tell you that. As a matter of fact a lot of unbelievable things have happened on this mission."

"Yes sir, I've noticed."

The Lt. Commander, the Chief and the Security Officer had formed a military inquiry of sorts. They were accusing Dr. Maccoby of contributing to the disappearance of Captain Young.

"But you were the last to see the Captain, isn't that right Doctor?" asked the Lt. Commander.

"I saw the Captain last night, she complained of sleeping problems but I don't know if I was the last to see her or not," answered Dr. Maccoby. "The Captain and I talked often, I think she felt comfortable discussing the days events with me. She had no one else."

"I see," said Lt. Commander Rollins. "Dr. Maccoby I also understand that you may have been the last to see Grace Parker alive. Were you aware of that?"

"No, I wasn't. But Grace was another person who needed a professional ear. I'm a trained psychiatrist you now."

"Yes I was aware of that Doctor," said Rollins. "Would it be possible for us to know what you discussed with Grace?"

"Well some of it is privileged," said Dr. Maccoby. "But it was pretty much the same things I discussed with the Captain."

"But Grace Patrick, unlike Captain Young, had several other friends she could rely upon, didn't she?"

"Yes of course but there are some things that a person feels more comfortable with discussing with a trained professional rather than a friend."

"I see. Now doctor isn't it true that you prescribed an aerosol for Grace Patrick?"

"Yes that's true."

"And what was in that aerosol?"

"Just a mild sedative."

"Delivered by nanobots?"

"Of course, it was targeted to certain areas of the body. In that way the side-effects of such drugs are eliminated."

"Of course doctor, that is understandable but I think we have established one thing in both cases."

"Cases?"

"Yes Doctor you see although we had publicly attributed Grace Patrick's death to natural causes we continue to carry it officially as an unresolved case. And the one thing we have established in both cases is that you were the last to see either woman.

"You also have the means to effect the death of Grace Patrick, that is the nano-machinery that you have access to as a doctor aboard this ship and admit using. And we know from your records that you know how to re-program the nano-machinery. I believe one of your doctorates was in nano-medicine, is that not correct?"

"Yes Lt. Commander but if I may ask, exactly what are you trying to say?"

"I'm saying that we have recorded evidence of the facts as I've stated them. And I am saying that you are the top suspect in the deaths of both of these women."

"The Captain has been found dead?"

"Not yet."

"And my motive Lt. Commander?"

"That Dr. Maccoby is the only reason this is an inquiry and not a tribunal. You are free to go, for now."

Dr. Maccoby rose slowly staring at the Lt. Commander, then turned and walked out of the room without another word.

Once they were alone Rollins swore under his breath. The other two men looked at him with concern.

"We still haven't a motive."

He turned to Lt. Aaron.

"I'm going out on a limb here Lieutenant. Are you sure you can follow her no matter what?"

"Yes Lt. Commander I assure you," said Security Officer Aaron quickly but not reassuringly.

While most of the others were out physically searching for Captain Young. Jerome was taking a different tack. Instead of physically searching Jerome was searching the ship's computer net. Something was going on and since no person had been found to be at fault perhaps it wasn't a person.

He had breached the security protocols and had his Emmie going through the logs. This wasn't as illegal as it sounded because Jerome had responsibility for maintaining those protocols. Breaching them was just his way of testing the system. He had done it several times to make sure he could find such a breach if it occurred.

The Emmie when finished brought up a few exceptions that it needed Jerome's help to deal with. The robotic fueling arm and video surveillance of the area he expected to see but there were a few more that he didn't expect.

One of the gaps was in the security video of the hallway outside the Captain's quarters. The last thing it showed was Dr. Maccoby leaving the quarters, then a gap of five minutes or so until the recording began again. The other gap was in the security monitors outside of Grace Parker's quarters the night of her death.

Impossible. The security Emmies would have alerted to such gaps as soon as they occurred.

Jerome then searched for one more unexplained gap. A gap that wasn't correlated to equipment failure or a recording dropout which happened from time to time. And he found it. The security camera outside one of the safe rooms behind the front shield of the ship. Protected by the thick meta-material and surrounding magnetic field the safe rooms were for crew protection should the ship be caught in a particle storm.

Jerome now knew the location of the Captain. And he thought he knew what was behind all the incidents. Then he heard the alarm. It was a storm warning.

How ironic.

But he didn't move immediately to evacuate to a safe room. First he had to cut all communication conduits into and out of those rooms.

9

"You did what engineer?" bellowed the Lt. Commander.

Just my luck assigned to the same room as the brass, thought Jerome.

"I disabled all communications between the safe rooms and the rest of the ship sir."

"You idiot, how are we supposed to monitor the flare storm or for that matter monitor the ship? Did you think about that?"

"Sir, the ship is on auto."

"Even so engineer we are now deaf and blind. When we get out of this I'll be sure that you are charged with endangering this mission and its crew."

"Sir, as far as monitoring the flare storm we can do that directly from here. Hear that sound?"

Everyone was quiet. The sound was like the buzzing of high-voltage lines in the summertime back on Earth.

"That sound," continued Jerome, "is the magnetic field generator located just next to these rooms. It is under strain now as the particles from the flare storm of WISE 0536 hit the magnetic field and cause it to warp. When we can no longer hear that sound it will be safe to send a bot out and get a particle and x-ray reading."

"I see," said the Lt. Commander feeling somewhat chastised. "I apologize for my tone of voice engineer but still you haven't told me why you cut our communication's channels?"

"To keep it out."

"Keep what out engineer," said Rollins somewhat exasperated.

"Sir I believe we have a rogue AGI aboard."

"AGI?" asked one of the men.

"Yes an Artificial General Intelligence."

"An Aggie?" asked the same crewman.

"Yes an Aggie has been the cause of all the incidents. That is the only explanation that makes sense for all the security breaches I have just discovered."

"You mean the loss of security vids?" asked Rollins.

"Yes sir."

"And the death of Grace Patrick and the Captain missing?"

"Yes sir. But I expect the Captain is still alive and in one of the safe rooms, though not this one apparently."

The Artificial General Intelligences or Aggies had not been around nearly as long as the Ems. Aggies were primarily found in the Solar System and only recently in the Centauri System. Because their background was from computer science, not a scanned human brain, Aggies didn't have a rapport with people.

They were generally found in research labs or the employment of governments or large corporations.

The Aggies essentially ran the Solar System as the governments there had turned over most functions to them. In return the Earth, Mars and others ran very efficiently. Many thought it a golden age. The Aggies could control many diseases, the more severe weather events and even the vagaries of humanity.

But now for some reason there was an Aggie on the *Daedalus Unbound* that no one had even suspected. Not even the person that had brought it aboard. And Aggies had the capability to reprogram nano-tech to anything they wanted. They could do the same with Emmies and lesser intelligences such as the one that controlled the robotic arm.

But right now the Aggie aboard the *Daedalus* was enraged, if Aggies could feel enraged. The AGI was quickly searching for a safe place to ride out the flare event. But time was running out and systems all over the ship were shutting down to prepare for the worst of the storm.

The Aggie could already see its escape routes being cut one by one. The first was the safe rooms. They had gone offline almost immediately. It didn't make sense to the Aggie, that wasn't protocol.

But there wasn't time right now to figure it out as one system after another powered down. The Aggie was being squeezed, its resources limited. It was losing some of its remote capabilities, it was retreating to its core. It successfully prevented the system containing its core from going offline but that was only a brief reprieve.

The high energy particles from the flare were impinging on the ship now. Without a magnetic shield the electronics the Aggie was in were being sliced up and crippled as if by a shower of bullets. The Aggie was now losing core capabilities such as memory and cognition. It was impossible to stop, impossible to defend against. The Aggie was reduced to a simpleton and then nothing.

It was four hours until the whine of the magnetic generator relented. The Lt. Commander sent a bot out capable of reading the space weather of particles and x-rays. It reported back a high but diminishing reading. Every thirty minutes the bot went out for a reading. After the third foray its particle counters showed a reading low enough for people to venture out.

The Lt. Commander sent the engineers and support personnel to restart systems. He sent one of the crew around to the other safe rooms to account for their occupants. The crewman came back to report that the Captain had been found in one of the other safe rooms unconscious but apparently okay. She was with the doctors including Dr. Maccoby. It wasn't long until communications were restored and the settlers and rest of the crew were on their way from the safe rooms to the crew wheel.

The Captain felt somewhat shaky as she descended the ladder from the ship's spine into the rotating crew wheel. The gravity was increasing at each step. She would have liked to rest in her quarters but after a quick change of uniform and cleanup she was presiding over the meeting of her top officers and the engineers.

"Before we begin, Lt. Commander will you please give us a status report," asked the Captain.

"Captain we have restored almost all computer functions except the aft area which were partially destroyed. Those were given to Dr. Jackson to study. Otherwise we have nominal operation of all systems."

"Thank you Lt. Commander. Dr. Jackson do you have a report on the aft area electronics?"

"Only preliminary ma'am. The electronics from that area have been damaged. They appear not to have shutdown as is usual during a storm but were kept running by what I think was the AGI."

"Yes, the AI," said the Chief. "You have found definitive proof?"

"Not direct Chief but indirect. As I said the electronics module should have shut down during the storm but something kept it from doing so. I doubt it was a glitch in the software as all other systems on the ship did shutdown."

"So we don't actually know that an AGI was onboard the *Daedalus* since we started this mission?" asked the Captain.

"I would say that I am about ninety percent sure ma'am," said Jerome. "And I have requested through our wormhole communications channel an update from Centauri on any unusual activities that the AGI's there or on Earth have taken."

“Very well Dr. Jackson I will be waiting for a further report when you have something more concrete,” said the Captain. “Chief how about the mission? Are we ready to continue?”

“A couple more days to recharge the isotopics and we can make the next jump ma'am.”

“Okay the engineers and others may go. I would like the Chief and Lt. Commander to remain.”

After the others had left the Captain began, “Gentlemen as you might expect Dr. Maccoby is a bit upset about the way she was treated just before the flare storm.”

“Yes ma'am I understand I intend to apologize directly,” said the Lt. Commander.

“You too Chief?”

“Yes ma'am.”

“But,” said the Lt. Commander. “The Chief and I were trying desperately to find you before it was too late. Dr. Maccoby was the best suspect we could come up with at the time. That is why we pressured her, hoping that she would make a move that would lead us to you and also solve Grace Patrick's murder.”

“Yes ma'am,” said the Chief. “We felt that time was short and we had to do something if we were going to find you alive.”

“I understand gentlemen and I believe if you make a sincere apology to the Doctor and explain your actions we may be able to put this incident behind us. Hopefully engineer Jackson will come through with some solid evidence that an AGI was at the root of our troubles."

The Lt. Commander and Chief both nodded.

"Very well, thank you gentlemen."

The Captain rose and left the room bound for her quarters where she could get the long rest she needed before the next wormhole jump.

10

It was the following day at fourteen-hundred hours that Jerome received a reply to his message. Glynn Kranz the Mission Director still had some contacts on Titan that knew through business connections what was happening in the inner Solar System where the Aggies were mostly located.

It turned out that almost all communications with Earth and most with Mars had been recently lost. Before that happened the contacts on Titan had received a briefing from their business partners that their dealings might be temporarily interrupted by what was happening with the Aggies.

It seemed the Aggies had started acting irregularly some months before. Nothing alarming at the time but their behavior became more and more erratic. Aggies had stopped most of the trade in the Solar System and between the Solar System and Centauri System. Such a move endangered billions of lives and made no sense to the business associates. A movement had started to supersede the Aggies management.

But it was slow in gaining traction because so much of the management of the economies and governments had been turned over to the Aggies. The final report from the business associates had talked about millions starving and the meta-verse, where humans could escape into a Aggie created virtual world, being destroyed. The infrastructure supporting the Aggies was being dismantled by militaries and mobs as fast as possible. Old fission weapons had been used, by which side was unclear, and then the reports had stopped.

Centauri System had quarantined the few Aggies in the system. They were recommending that all Aggies be quarantined.

Jerome smiled.

As if I didn't know. This latest information should convince anyone that had doubts about what had caused the incidences aboard and it should also convince them to continue the mission.

He would tell the Captain but first he would tell Lauren. She had been worried too long, he didn't like her to worry so.

ABOUT THE AUTHOR

D.W. Patterson lives in the USA with his beautiful wife Sarah. He studied physics and read classic science fiction in college and then worked for many years as an electronic design engineer.

Now he's trying to write stories like the ones he once loved. See his website dwpatterson.com for more information.

Hard Science Fiction – Old School.

Also By This Author:

The Future Chron Universe:

To date the Future Chron Universe has:

51 Amazon Top 100's

(15 in the Top 10)

In chronological order.

Volume numbers indicate Universe order.

Book numbers indicate Series order.

From The Earth Series

(Novellas except where noted):

Volume 1, Book 1 – *Whatsoever You Do*

Volume 2, Book 2 – *War Through The Pines*

Volume 3, Book 3 – *Vigilance*

Volume 4, Book 4 – *To Tend And Watch Over*

Volume 5, Book 5 – *Union*

Volume 6, Book 6 – *Circle Of Retribution*

Volume 7, Book 7 – *Freedom From Want*

Volume 8, Book 8 – *Break Up*

Volume 9, Book 9 – *Kuiper Station*

Volume 10, Book 10 – *The Cloud*

Volume 11, Book 11 – *First Interstellar* – A Short Novel

Wormhole Series

(Novels):

Volume 12, Book 1 – *Mach's Metric*

Volume 13, Book 2 – *Mach's Mission*

Open Space Series

(Short Stories):

Volume 14, Book 1 – *Open Space*

Volume 15, Book 2 – *The Old World*

Volume 16, Book 3 – *Insurrect*

Volume 17, Book 4 – *Second Beam*

Volume 18, Book 5 – *All For One*

Volume 19, Book 6 – *One For All*

Volume 20, Book 7 – *Shotgun*

Volume 21, Book 8 – *Allison*

To The Stars Series

(Novellas):

Volume 22, Book 1 – *First One Hundred*

Volume 23, Book 2 – *First Dark Ages*

Volume 24, Book 3 – *Second One Hundred*

Volume 25, Book 4 – *Second Dark Ages*

Volume 26, Book 5 – *Path Of The Long March*

Wormhole Series

(Novel):

Volume 27, Book 3 – *Mach's Legacy*

Robot Series

(Novels):

Volume 28, Book 1 – *Spin-Two*

Volume 29, Book 2 – *Robot Planet*

Volume 30, Book 3 – *The Lattice Of Space*

Time Series

(Novels):

Volume 31, Book 1 – *Time Wars*

Volume 32, Book 2 – *Time's End*

Volume 33, Book 3 – *Frozen Time*

The Remembered Earth Universe:

To date the Remembered Earth Universe has:

8 Amazon Top 100's

Cislunar Series

(Short Stories):

Volume 1, Book 1 – *US Tugs*

Volume 2, Book 2 – *Prototype*

Volume 3, Book 3 – *L1 Or Bust*

Volume 4, Book 4 – *Guidance Box*

Volume 5, Book 5 – *Air Brakes*

Volume 6, Book 6 – *View Point*

Volume 7, Book 7 – *Space Truck*

Volume 8, Book 8 – *Dark Side* – *In Progress*

The Manifold Earth Universe:

Volume 1, Book 1 – *The Realm* – *In Progress*

Don't miss out!

Visit the website below and you can sign up to receive emails whenever D.W. Patterson publishes a new book. There's no charge and no obligation.

https://books2read.com/r/B-A-DPWE-HAIJC

BOOKS 2 READ

Connecting independent readers to independent writers.

www.ingramcontent.com/pod-product-compliance
Lightning Source LLC
LaVergne TN
LVHW010501160826
845677LV00012B/2583